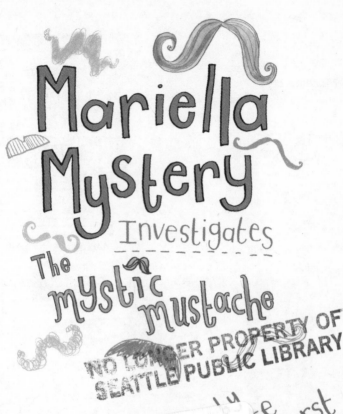

Mariella Mystery

Investigates

The Mystic Mustache

by
...nkhurst

D0950235

Never miss a clue!

Join our **Mariella Mystery Investigates Club** for the latest news on your favorite sleuth-y detective, plus:

- A club certificate and membership card
- **Mariella Mystery** games, activities, puzzles, and coloring pages
- Excerpts from the books and news about forthcoming titles
- Contests for **FREE** stuff

You can become the next Young Super Sleuth—just like Mariella!

Visit **barronsbooks.com/mariella/** today and join in the fun!

Open to U.S. residents only.

Look out for more books about Mariella Mystery

A Cupcake Conundrum
The Disappearance of
   Diana Dumpling
The Ghostly Guinea Pig
The Huge Hair Scare

A Kitty Calamity
The Mystery of the Cursed Poodle
The Mystic Mustache
The Spaghetti Yeti

Mariella Mystery

Investigates

The Mystic Mustache

by Kate Pankhurst

BARRON'S

For Jenny Glencross,
a true Mystery Girl!

my
mustache
collection

THIS YOUNG SUPER SLEUTH JOURNAL BELONGS TO . . .

Mariella Mystery, that's me. Totally amazing girl detective, aged nine and three quarters.

I'm serious about being the best young detective ever, that's why I've been working hard to extend my collection of fake mustaches. A good detective has a mustache for every mystery situation.

NOTE: Arthur—singing on the toilet is not a mystery situation, and is definitely not the place to wear your sister's best and bushiest mustache. Do not do that again. EVER.

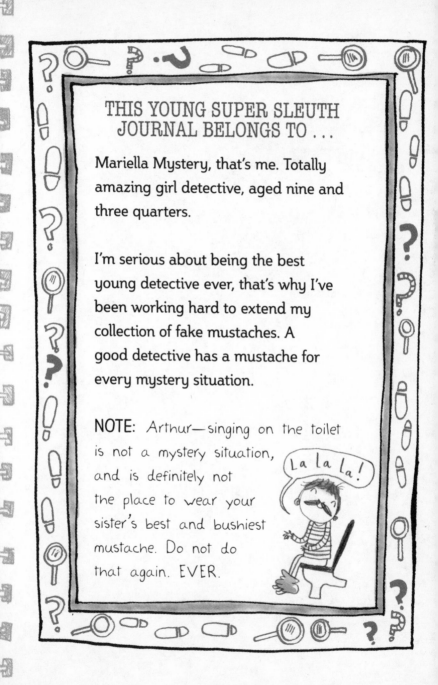

La la la!

The Young Super Sleuth's Society Presents

THE YOUNG SUPER SLEUTHER COMPETITION & CONVENTION

Calling all Young Super Sleuths!

MYSTIC MUSTACHE MAYHEM!
Witness the talents of the best Young Super Sleuths as they compete to become this year's Young Super Sleuther Champion.

TOP SECRET!
Uncover classified information about famous detectives and infamous master criminals in the Young Super Sleuth Experience.

THRILLS!
Ride the Bone Rattler, search the Gruesome Crime Scene Investigation Area, and survive the Bumper Cars of Bafflement! (If you dare.)

LOCATION: Known Mystery Hot Spot, the town of Puddleford, Puddleford Park.

DATES: Monday, August 6th–Thursday, August 9th

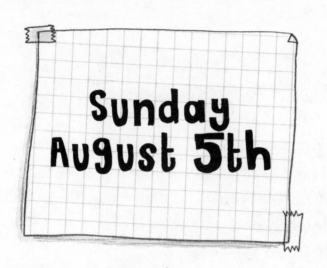

Sunday August 5th

NOTE: Poppy has finished our competition outfits, ready for tomorrow! Eeeek! I'm so excited. Having a distinct Mystery Style is an important part of looking like the Young Super Sleuther champions we want to become.

cool hats

yellow trench coats

2:15 PM
PUDDLEFORD PARK, FINAL MYSTERY GIRL YOUNG SUPER SLEUTHER PRACTICE SESSION COMPLETE

I can totally imagine it. Crowds cheering and cameras flashing as Young Super Sleuther winners—the Mystery Girls—are presented with the gleaming golden Mystic Mustache trophy.

Or I *could* totally imagine it—until our last practice session, which did not go according to plan.

OPERATION WIN MYSTIC MUSTACHE

THE TEAM:

VIOLET MAPLE: Mystery Girl with an eye for detail—has checked that our Mystery Kit contains everything we need fifty-seven times. (Good thing she did, or we would have forgotten to pack fake mustache glue.)

Violet searching the mystery kit

mustache glue

Poppy and her magnifying glass

POPPY HOLMES: Mystery Girl on a mission to win! I bet none of the other teams had a preparation schedule like the one Poppy designed. She says we can't be sure what mystery-solving challenges we'll face, so the only way to win is to be good at everything.

THE SCHEDULE

MARIELLA MYSTERY (ME):

Mystery Girl with her eyes on the Mystic Mustache trophy. I just need to stay calm when the competition gets tough and remember that I am a brilliant detective.

me, with my cool hat

TARGET: THE MYSTIC MUSTACHE

The trophy is famous (and not just in the detective world) because so many of the young detectives who have won

The Mystic Mustache

it have gone on to solve high-profile mysteries and become famous. It's worth millions because it's made from a block of gold presented to the Young Super Sleuth Society seventy years ago, for catching the Bejeweled Bandit (stole jewels from movie stars).

Bejeweled Bandit

12

TASK: UNDERCOVER SURVEILLANCE SKILLS

1:00 PM: As planned, the Mystery Girls rendezvous* at Puddleford Park on our bikes to practice undercover surveillance on park users.

Our bikes

*RENDEZVOUS: A French word, which sophisticated detectives like us use. It's a fancy way of saying meeting up.

1:01 PM: We stop to take a look at the enormous Young Super Sleuther tents being set up behind a fence in the center of the park, knowing that tomorrow we won't be practicing— we'll be competing for real.

1:02 PM: The serious moment is ruined when a familiar squeaky voice shrieks from the park entrance—"MARIELLAAAA! WAIT FOR MEEEEEE! I WANT TO JOIN IN!"

ARTHUR MYSTERY:

Annoying younger brother who is desperate to be a Mystery Girl. (He never will be.) I told Mom and Dad that the Mystery Girls need to prepare for the competition, but they insisted on bringing along Arthur for a nice picnic.

arthur. Being annoying

I don't have time for sausage rolls—and I definitely don't have time for Arthur!

1:06 PM: Poppy says that Arthur might be quite useful. What is she talking about? There is no way we can perfect our undercover surveillance techniques (which involves a lot of sneaking around quietly) with Arthur here.

Annoying

1:07 PM: Poppy tells Arthur his task is to try and escape from us on his scooter so we can practice a high-speed chase situation.

1:08 PM: We let Arthur have a head start—as far as the swings—before we follow him.

1:11 PM: Arthur is screaming, "I'M A MYSTERY GIRL, WHEEEEEEE!" We must catch him.

1:15 PM: Wind whooshes in my ears and my legs burn. Arthur is surprisingly fast. I hear Mom shout in the distance that we need to slow down. Never.

1:16 PM: Without warning, Arthur's brakes screech and he stops in front of us, next to an ice cream truck. Violet and Poppy scream. I slam on my brakes, but it's too late.

ice cream

1:18 PM: We CRASH into the side of the ice cream truck. Bottles of raspberry sauce and sprinkles topple from the freezer onto our heads. Arthur shouts, "MOMMMM! CAN I HAVE AN ICE POP?"

1:19 PM: Before I can untangle myself from my bike, on the road outside the park I see an official-looking black van approaching. I realize, with horror, that it has the Young Super Sleuth Society logo on the side.

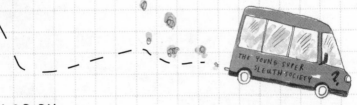

1:20 PM: I hope nobody guesses we are competitors (no serious detective walks around with sprinkles in his or her hair), but our bright yellow detective coats are a huge giveaway.

1:21 PM: I see for the first time the faces of the rival young detective agencies we'll be competing against. Most stare at us, puzzled, but two boys snicker from the back window of the van as it passes.

1:22 PM: Final Young Super Sleuther practice session abandoned. Operation Emergency Clean Up Mystery Outfits Using Mom's Wet Wipes commences.

LEVEL OF COMPETITION READINESS: WINNERS DON'T LET STUFF LIKE THIS HAPPEN! WE ARE PROCEEDING INTO THE FIRST COMPETITION CHALLENGE WITH EXTREME CAUTION.

NOTE: Hopefully this was just an Arthur-related glitch. (Never, ever let Arthur join in with Mystery Girl activity.)

WORKING IN PARTNERSHIP

Certain mystery situations, such as those spanning a large geographical area or requiring specialist skills you do not have, may be best solved by joining forces with another young detective agency. Getting used to the way that others work can be tricky—don't let a potentially perfect partnership end up being an awful association.

Let's see if you are as good as you say you are.

Hey, partner.

Teamwork: Top Tips

Using a **secret handshake** can be a great way to cement friendships between detective agencies.

I know a MUCH better way to do it.

Others may have **different investigative methods** than you, but that doesn't mean that they are wrong. Avoid being discouraging.

Rivalry can ruin relationships. Instead of getting jealous, see what you can learn from each other.

I've solved more cases than you.

Mom says I've got to be home for dinner by 7 pm.

Be **understanding** that other young detectives may have different schedules than the ones you are used to.

Respect privacy. Do not search your partner agency's Mystery HQ while they are in the bathroom. Nobody likes a busybody.

WARNING

Not all young detective agencies have good intentions when they seek to work with you. In rare cases they may wish to spy on you in order to steal ideas, or because they work for an enemy! Remain vigilant.

HA HA! They don't suspect a thing!

my bedroom

6:15 PM
MY BEDROOM, MY HOUSE, 22 SYCAMORE AVENUE

Once we'd cleaned most of the raspberry sauce from our outfits, Poppy calmed down and said that it's fine that we didn't meet our competition rivals looking cool and mysterious because now they might believe we aren't much of a threat. Little do they know that—most of the time—we are totally amazing detectives.

We are cool and mysterious

The Young Super Sleuth's Handbook does say that if things have gone well for a while, like our other practice sessions have, it can make you complacent.*

*COMPLACENT: Thinking, well, I've been amazing at creative disguises, undercover surveillance, clue detection, and gadget design, so of course we'll win the competition, when actually you can't relax—not even for a second—because the Young Super Sleuther competition will throw something at you that will blow your Mystery Senses into a million squiggly pieces.

my mystery senses

Whenever I find myself worrying about whether our detective skills won't be as good as the other competitors', I have to remind myself that 703 young detective agencies entered the competition. Only five were selected—and one of them was us!

Three weeks ago, the Young Super Sleuth's Society called to say we placed and that our application form really stood out!

(I had a spooky moment and totally knew the second the phone rang it would be about the competition. Dad says that's because I'd thought every phone call since mailing our application form was going to be the Young Super Sleuth's Society. But I'm still taking it as a good sign that my Mystery Senses are working well.)

intriguing evidence

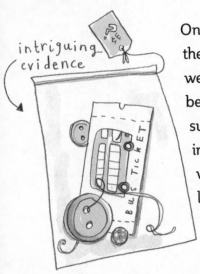

On the form we'd listed all the complicated mysteries we've solved (there have been lots now), and made sure we included some intriguing evidence, along with pictures of ourselves looking highly professional.

Every year, the Young Super Sleuth's Society chooses the hometown of one of its members to host their competition and convention, so we provided information and newspaper clippings about mysterious locations we'd investigated in Puddleford.

In fact, thinking about it, I can't believe I was surprised when the Young Super Sleuth's Society agreed that Puddleford was the perfect place to host the event!

MYSTERIOUS LOCATIONS IN PUDDLEFORD

Sinister swing

Puddleford Theater

EMPTY HOUSE

gardens

Deserted Path

dreadful dumpster

Hang on—Mom's calling me for dinner. The Young Super Sleuth's Handbook says that an empty stomach can lead to a loss of focus. I can't risk that before tomorrow.

my Dinner

broccoli
Potato
Sausage
Peas

6:45 PM
MY BEDROOM, AGAIN

I only managed to eat half a sausage and a piece
of broccoli at dinner because I felt so nervous
and excited all at the same time.

I've read about previous Young Super Sleuther
competitions in the Young Super Sleuth's
Newsletter. The challenges sound totally difficult,
but they also sound totally mysterious. Every
day I wake up hoping something mysterious
will happen to me, so these could be the most
amazing four days of my life!

The thing I'm most looking forward to is the Expect the Unexpected Challenge. That's where the judges test the contestants' absolute limit with a surprise task. You'd think contestants would get better at expecting something unexpected is going to happen—that's what being a detective is all about—but it always seems to catch them off guard.

Last year, during a challenge to search a haunted house, each detective agency had a member unexpectedly kidnapped. They had to investigate the paranormal activity and find out what had happened to their missing team members.

Realistic
haunted
house

Wooooooh

awoooh!

One detective couldn't handle it and was found wrapped in a shower curtain in the bathtub, squeaking that he didn't want to be a detective anymore.

traumatized

I'd like to think nothing like that would ever happen to a Mystery Girl, but Violet says even the most advanced young detectives can go to pieces when their every move is being watched by a massive audience and superstar detective judges.

SUPERSTAR JUDGES

ELLE LUSIVE: Known as the Mystery Mover, she is famed for combining gymnastics and disguise. When she isn't undercover, she wears a sparkly jumpsuit, just in case she has to do acrobatics to chase down a criminal or cartwheel to the scene of a crime.

Elle Lusive being bendy

Tartania McSnuff

TARTANIA MCSNUFF: Scottish detective who specializes in mysterious creatures, she is reported to have come close to catching the Loch Ness Monster. Wow. I hope she's designed some challenges that involve looking for mysterious creatures.

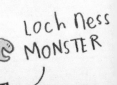

Loch Ness MONSTER

Elle and Tartania are past winners of the Mystic Mustache and they are AMAZING detectives. I hope the Mystery Girls can follow in their footsteps.

We won't be able to bring the actual Mystic Mustache home if we win—because it's so valuable, and being young detectives, we don't have the right level of security in our HQ to make sure nobody steals it. Instead, our names will be etched into the trophy and then we will bring home a very realistic rubber replica that we can put on display.

Until then, I've drawn a life-size picture of it and hung it next to my bed to focus my mystery-solving mind.

The mystic mustache

9:30 AM
YOUNG SUPER SLEUTHER COMPETITION AND
CONVENTION SITE, PUDDLEFORD PARK

WE ARE HERE! This is actually happening!

Walking into the competition site was like
entering a dream world of mysteriousness.
Terrified screams filled the air (from the Bone
Rattler Ride in the Zone of Mystery) and a sea of
shimmering, golden, mustache-shaped, helium
balloons bobbed above the heads of the crowd.

Poppy, Violet, and I had just
enough time before the first
challenge to hurry through the
Young Super Sleuth Experience
Tent and catch a glimpse of the
Mystic Mustache trophy.

We knew we must be close because a
massive crowd had gathered in a small,
very dark room and there was lots of oohing
and ahhing. The crowd might not have been
detectives, but I could understand why they
were so excited. It's not every day that a piece
of mystery-solving history like this comes to
Puddleford. (Or that we get the chance to win it!)

I pushed my way to the front, pulling
Poppy and Violet with me, and
managed to get around the
security guard who was telling
people to stay behind the rope.

The trophy stood in a huge glass display case, like a very fancy goldfish in a tank. Spotlights shined on it, and beams of light twinkled from the points of the twirly mustache. If you looked really closely, you could see the tiny names of winners carved into its base.

That's when it felt real. That's when I realized just how huge it would be for the Mystery Girls' names to be on that trophy. (That's also when I felt sick because my tummy started doing nervous cartwheels, like the kind Elle Lusive can do.)

10:45 AM
YOUNG SUPER SLEUTHER BACKSTAGE AREA,
MEETING OUR COMPETITION RIVALS

I think I'm doing an OK job of making it look as
if I'm cool and collected, even though I am in a
room filled with the country's best young detective
agencies.

When Elle Lusive and Tartania McSnuff introduced
themselves, my tummy did the biggest acrobatic
backflip so far.

sparkly

Plaid
(mystery
kit

"Helloo, competitors," said Tartania in her soft Scottish accent. "Seeing you all waiting to start your Young Super Sleuther journey brings back happy memories."

"Ah, yes, winning the Mystic Mustache was one of the best moments of my life too," said Elle, grinning. "Now I hope you're feeling ready for the challenges ahead? There's nothing to be nervous about. Is there, Tartania?"

Poppy nudged me. Violet looked terrified. They both knew that what Elle actually meant was: *You should be nervous, very nervous.*

Worried

After that, Elle and Tartania left to prepare for the first challenge and told everyone to get to know one another. It was an excellent opportunity to check out the competition. Here's who we are up against:

THE COMPETITORS

THE BAFFLEMENT BOYS:

Linus and Pip. I suspected they were going to be trouble when they laughed at us yesterday. Linus said, "Oh, when we saw you in the park, we assumed you must be amateurs, not competitors."

Bafflement Boys

WHAT? Just because they can do a really good Mystery Eyebrow* does not mean they are better detectives than us.

BEST MYSTERY EVER SOLVED: Prevented the theft of a priceless spoon from their local art gallery. A spoon? Doesn't sound that impressive.

Spoon

*****MYSTERY EYEBROW:** Using your eyebrows to look ultra-suspicious. I can do this, but only for short periods of time. Pip's and Linus's eyebrows seem to be fixed in that position.

mystery eyebrow

THE SUSPICIOUS SISTAS: Manesha, Kiki, and Dot. Not actually sisters and they don't seem that suspicious, they seemed more interested in high-fiving us and shouting, "GO, SISTA!" really loudly.

matching glittery hoodies

The Suspicious Sistas

BEST MYSTERY EVER SOLVED: Revealed that a haunted shoe shop was not haunted at all. It was just the shop owners trying to attract attention by levitating stilettos on invisible thread. (Doesn't sound too difficult.)

haunted stilettos

DARLENE DANGERFIELD:

Didn't smile once, and annoyingly, she's managed to get the rare Young Super Sleuth badge that says, "DANGER IS MY MIDDLE NAME." (Well, it's not, it's her last name.)

Darlene looking moody

DANGER IS MY MIDDLE NAME

BEST MYSTERY EVER SOLVED: Refused to tell us! Said it was top-secret information. Hmmm. More like she hasn't ever solved any decent mysteries.

Jess, Ben, and Bobby

GIVE US A CLUE: Jess, Ben, and Bobby. They aren't much older than Arthur, so can't be a real threat. Even so, Violet says we shouldn't underestimate them.

BEST MYSTERY EVER SOLVED: Exposed a child in their class who was stealing crayons in all the best colors—silver, gold, and fluorescent pink. Simple stuff.

Crayons

refreshments

Juice

2:05 PM
YOUNG SUPER SLEUTHER BACKSTAGE AREA,
BREAK TIME. FIRST CHALLENGE COMPLETE

Tartania and Elle have called a short break
because they can't decide who should win the
first challenge. I don't think it will be us.

"Contestants," Elle said, when we were all lined
up on stage. "Your first Super Sleuther Challenge
is . . ."

My heart raced. All of Puddleford was expecting to
see stunning detective work.

". . . to build a Mystery HQ suitable for a detective agency serious about becoming a Super Sleuther Champion. You have three hours. GO!" Tartania continued.

Lights flashed and a heavy black curtain behind us lifted, revealing five rooms, one for each team. There were sparkling silver containers lined up in front of the rooms, overflowing with furniture, fabric, and detective equipment.

Even though I know a lot of stuff about what a HQ should have in it, because we spent a long time perfecting the real Mystery Girl HQ, I had the sudden feeling that I had completely forgotten it all. Linus from the Bafflement Boys didn't hesitate. He dashed past us, grabbed a lamp from one of the containers and sprinted into their HQ.

Everything happened in a blur. The audience cheered; Poppy grabbed equipment while I arranged it; Violet shouted out things we have in Mystery Girl HQ: "INTRUDER ALERT! QUIET ZONE! EVIDENCE INSPECTION TABLE!"

When the announcement came that the challenge was complete I had to tell myself to breathe —our HQ looked totally amazing, just like the real Mystery Girl HQ does. We had a cool old-fashioned mystery desk and a huge bulletin board. But . . .

"WHERE did the Suspicious Sistas get that hammock?" Poppy said, staring at their beach-themed relaxation zone. "I'm sure we've done enough . . . OH NO!"

Beach-themed relaxation zone

Poppy pointed at the Bafflement Boys' HQ next.

They'd managed to build an enormous bookshelf neatly stacked with items from their super-cool gadget collection. I couldn't believe I'd thought our beanbag chill-out zone would be enough!

Looking at the amazing touches in the other rooms, I got a horrible sinking feeling that our ideas just weren't as good.

Any minute now we'll have to go back out there. What if we come in last?

Darlene's concealed hiding place

Give Us a Clue's door

GIVE US a CLUE

DETECTIVE AGENCY

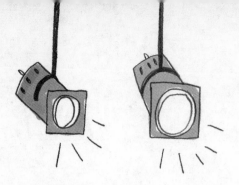

2:20 PM
YOUNG SUPER SLEUTHER COMPETITION
STAGE. IN CHAOS

I was ready to expect the unexpected, but I don't
think anybody was prepared for what has just
happened! (And I'm not talking about who won
the first challenge.)

Returning to the stage to hear the results, I
hoped we looked as professional as Tartania
did. Elle Lusive wasn't with her, but I thought
maybe she was going to come on stage doing
a celebratory backflip when the winner was
announced or something.

"And the winners are
. . . The Suspicious
Sistas!" Tartania said.
"Well done, Sistas—the
beach is the perfect place to
think about whodunnit!!"

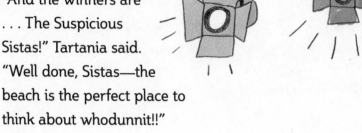

The Suspicious Sistas started dancing and high-fiving each other.

A leader board flashed up on the big screens at the side of the stage. The Bafflement Boys took second place (they did not look happy) and the Mystery Girls (phew) took third. Darlene Dangerfield came in fourth and looked furious. Give Us a Clue didn't take the news that they had come in last well. Bobby fell to the floor sobbing.

Anyway, none of that seems to matter. Not after what happened next.

Elle Lusive suddenly appeared on the big screens. She was cartwheeling toward us down the dark hallway in the Young Super Sleuth Experience.

"There's still everything to play for, competitors!" she said, flipping upright. "Now, I've got something to show you that will focus your Mystery Senses . . ." She tiptoed through the Young Super Sleuth Experience, as if she was on an undercover mission.

"I don't like this!" whispered Violet. "It's the Expect the Unexpected Challenge—I don't think I can handle anything else today."

But it wasn't that.

"This is what being a Young Super Sleuther is all about—THIS is what you are working for!" Elle said, beckoning the camera to follow her into the tiny dark room we'd visited this morning. "Behold, the world-famous Mystic Mus—"

Elle froze. An expression of dark suspicion flashed over her face. (It was exactly like the one I've tried to copy from pictures of her in the Young Super Sleuth's Newsletter.)

The camera jerked from Elle to the Mystic Mustache's fancy stand. Spotlights still shined above it, but now the only thing they lit up was a jagged hole in the glass display case.

I made an emergency detective deduction.

NEW MYSTERY ALERT: THE MYSTIC MUSTACHE HAS BEEN STOLEN!

Dark suspicion

KNOW YOUR CRIME: THEFT

Ensure you are familiar with the tell-tale signs indicating that a theft has occurred. Acting quickly means you can be following clues before a victim even realizes a treasured item has been stolen. (Everyone loves a detective who solves a crime before it's reported.)

Top Ten Signs a Theft Has Occurred:

1. Hysterical victim screaming they can't find their handbag/shoes/sofa.

2. Gap on wall of an art gallery.

3. Person sprinting while pushing an overflowing shopping cart.

4. Speeding ice cream truck (could be a getaway car).

5. Suspicious burglar alarm maintenance worker.

6. A surprisingly light diamond tiara (could be a fake).

7. A car full of sheep. (Sheep rustling)

8. A bike that no longer works as it should.

9. A distressed dog, may have been dog-napped.

awOOoh!

10. Discovering a bathtub full of money.

small fortune

TOP TIP Don't overreact. Somebody borrowing a small invaluable item, like a pencil sharpener, does not mean you need to launch a full criminal investigation.

2:45 PM
YOUNG SUPER SLEUTH COMPETITION STAGE,
MYSTERY HQ (THE ONE WE JUST BUILT).
EMERGENCY MYSTERY GIRL TEAM MEETING

It wasn't just me who deduced what had
happened to the Mystic Mustache. Gasps
rippled around the stage. The Suspicious Sistas'
smiles had been replaced with looks of deep
shock. Darlene Dangerfield was shouting at Give
Us a Clue to stop screaming.

Bobby
Hysterical

Annoyingly, the Bafflement Boys managed to keep the same I'm-a-serious-and-suspicious-detective expression they'd had all morning. They weren't doing anything useful, though. Poppy and Violet shot me a glance that said, Emergency Mystery Girl Team Meeting needed—NOW.

A crew member ran across the stage and whispered to Tartania. I knew things must be bad, because although Tartania has come face to face with the Loch Ness Monster, it took her a moment to compose herself enough to speak.

"I have been asked to inform you all that the entire Young Super Sleuth site is closing immediately," she said. "The disappearance of the Mystic Mustache is being investigated by Elle, and I am about to join her. We hope that the competition will continue as planned tomorrow, but a further announcement will be issued in due course."

The curtains closed, muffling the frantic gossiping of the audience. Crew members were ushering us backstage so parents could come and pick us up. The Bafflement Boys dashed off first. I hoped this was a sign they weren't perfect all the time and were actually desperate for a hug from their moms to get over the trauma of the missing Mustache. (The Mystery Girls are made of stronger stuff.)

Nobody noticed me, Poppy, and Violet duck into the HQ we'd just built. (The perfect place for an emergency Mystery Girl team meeting.)

"This is a disaster," Poppy said. "We only got third place—if the competition is canceled, all our hard work will be for nothing!"

I knew we were better than third place too, but I couldn't believe Poppy thought that was more important than the theft of a world-famous, priceless, golden mustache! (It was potentially the biggest mystery situation the Mystery Girls have ever faced.)

"We need to figure out who took the Mystic Mustache and get it back, or there might not even *be* a Young Super Sleuther Competition," I said.

"Yes, this could ruin the Young Super Sleuth Society's reputation!" Violet said. "They are meant to be the world's best young detective society and the Mystic Mustache has been stolen from under their noses! Embarrassing alert!"

I hadn't even thought of that, but Violet was right. The Young Super Sleuth's Society has taught us everything we know about mystery-solving. We can't stand by and let everyone  think they are amateurs. (Or that the Mystery Girls have been trained by amateurs!)

"Let's start with some logical explanations," I said.

The Young Super Sleuth's Handbook says that logical explanations should always come before rushing off to do anything else—they help you formulate a plan. Without a plan you are just people running around picking up random things from the floor.

Logical Explanations:

(Shocking But Possible) Explanation

One: A competitor stole the Mystic Mustache because he or she knows, deep down, that he or she is not good enough to win it. Could one of them have sneaked off during the bathroom break and hidden the trophy when the coast was clear? Under a bumper car? In his or her Mystery Kit?

Contestants who went to the bathroom at break

Pip

Jess

Darlene

manesha

But none of the other contestants' Mystery Kits looked noticeably heavy just now. And would any of them really want to risk their detective careers by stealing it? Would he or she attempt such a thing with totally amazing detectives Elle and Tartania watching?

heavy

(Probable) Explanation Two:

A master criminal stole the Mystic Mustache so he or she could sell it—or because he or she has a grudge against the Young Super Sleuth's Society.

The trophy is famous, so lots of people might want to steal it. Also The Young Super Sleuth's Society must have annoyed plenty of criminals over the years who want revenge. Our list could be quite long.

(Practically Impossible) Explanation Three:

Elle Lusive said that the day she won the Mystic Mustache was the best of her life. Maybe she's secretly always wanted it back? And stole it while the film crew wasn't looking?

Elle Lusive doesn't need the Mystic Mustache! She has won many trophies for her detective work and is at the top of her career!

VERDICT: Elle Lusive wasn't on her own for long enough to steal the Mustache and she has no motive, unlike other suspects. We can rule her out but we need more evidence to narrow our suspect list further. We need to search the scene for clues that could reveal the identity of the thief, or point to the current whereabouts of the Mustache.

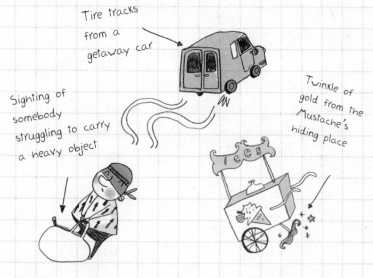

Tire tracks from a getaway car

Twinkle of gold from the Mustache's hiding place

Sighting of somebody struggling to carry a heavy object

NOTE: If the site is closed after today, the trail of clues could go cold—disaster! (We have to get started before Mom, Dad, and Arthur arrive backstage to take us home!)

3:30 PM
OUTSIDE THE YOUNG SUPER SLEUTH
EXPERIENCE TENT

We might have come in third in the Design a
Detective HQ Challenge, but I am awarding the
Mystery Girls first place for our excellent work on
Operation Explore the Experience.

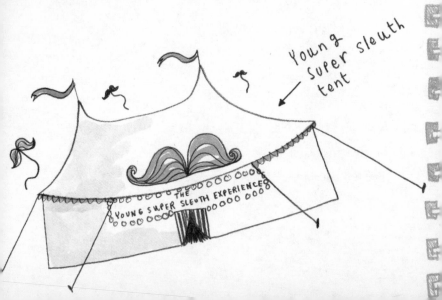

Young
super sleuth
tent

THE
YOUNG SUPER SLEUTH EXPERIENCE

3:00 PM: Outside the backstage exit of the competition stage, I spot Elle and Tartania in serious discussions with Detective Sparks from Puddleford Police. In high-profile cases, detective agencies often work in partnership with the police.

3:05 PM: Poppy, Violet, and I use the crowds shuffling toward the exit as cover, and run past an upturned balloon-seller's cart. Was this pushed over by the criminal as he or she escaped? Or a failed attempt to hide the Mustache?

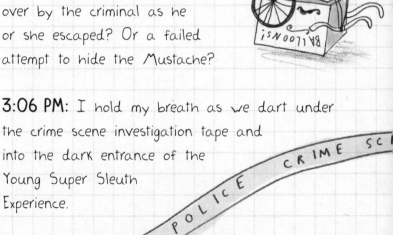

3:06 PM: I hold my breath as we dart under the crime scene investigation tape and into the dark entrance of the Young Super Sleuth Experience.

EVIDENCE UNCOVERED FROM MYSTIC MUSTACHE DISPLAY ROOM:

MYSTIC MUSTACHE DISPLAY
CASE: Glass is really thick so must have been smashed with a heavy object, like an iron or a brick or something. (No sign of anything like this.)

tea!

DISABLED ALARM SYSTEM: The alarm control wasn't working and had liquid all over it—a closer inspection revealed this to be milky tea. Does the thief drink tea?

GLITTERY YELLOW FLUFF: Could this have fallen from the Mustache-stealer's belly button?

fluff

wrapper

GOLDEN TAFFY TWISTER
WRAPPER: Is the thief a taffy eater, or was it dropped by a visitor?

58

3:15 PM: Footsteps approach. A flustered security guard—the same one who was guarding the trophy earlier—pokes his head around the door and asks what on earth we are doing.

3:16 PM: Poppy pretends to look really upset (good undercover work, Poppy) and says that we can't believe the Mystic Mustache is gone and we had to come and see it for ourselves.

3:18 PM: The security guard (badge says his name is Jim) looks at his feet. Then he says that it's all his fault and he can't believe he fell for a Classic Diversion Technique.* A Classic Diversion Technique? WHAT?!

*CLASSIC DIVERSION TECHNIQUE:
When a criminal does something, like tipping over a balloon-seller's cart, causing Jim to leave his post and investigate. Then, while the coast is clear, the criminal steals the Mystic Mustache!

VERDICT: Jim told us that the balloon cart was tipped over at approximately 2:00 PM— which means the Mystic Mustache went missing during the bathroom break after the Design a Detective HQ Challenge! So the

time of the crime

Mustache definitely could have been stolen by a competitor! Further analysis of the evidence is needed back at Mystery Girl HQ (the one at my house, not the one we've just built).

NOTE: We haven't found any sign of the Mystic Mustache hidden on the convention site. I asked the security guards at the park gates if they'd seen anyone suspicious. They said somebody could have danced past waving the Mystic Mustache and they wouldn't have noticed because they've been dealing with a crisis. (A mobility scooter is stuck in mud, blocking the exit to the parking lot everyone is now trying to leave.)

mud

flopped

Beanbag

5:30 PM
MYSTERY GIRL HQ. FLOPPED ON A BEANBAG

Ugh. We ended up in a traffic jam because of the stupid stuck mobility scooter.

stuck

Mom kept telling us that even if the competition was canceled, the Mystery Girls would always be winners in her eyes. Hmm. I'd definitely prefer to win the Mystic Mustache. I'm not sure it sounds very official if it's just my mom who thinks we are amazing detectives.

Back in HQ we had lots to discuss.

"It's disappointing that we can't narrow our suspect list yet," I said, "but now we know what time the Mustache was stolen, it confirms we need to keep investigating potential master criminals and other contestants."

Some contestants had the perfect Window of Opportunity* to commit the crime, after all.

*WINDOW OF OPPORTUNITY: A person can only do something terrible, like stealing the Mystic Mustache, if he or she isn't already busy doing something else. Sneaking off when everyone thinks you are in the bathroom, for example, is a perfect window of opportunity.

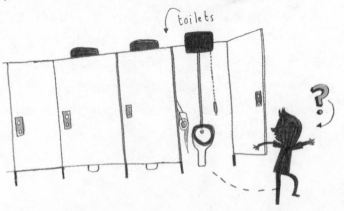

62

"You're right—we need to hope that the competition isn't canceled. If the site shuts down, important clues might be lost and investigating will get tricky," Violet said.

"Definitely," Poppy said. "Some of our prime suspects would be sent home—possibly with the Mystic Mustache!"

No matter what happens tomorrow, we can't leave this case unsolved. That's why we've looked at our current suspects in more detail—The Young Super Sleuth's Handbook says this is an excellent way to be sure you don't miss anything that could be important.

Turn over for suspect line-up

OUR SUSPECTS

PIP, BAFFLEMENT BOY:

Were he and Linus able to remain calm when they heard the Mystic Mustache had been stolen because they'd always planned for Pip to sneak off and steal it?

A CRAZED MASTER CRIMINAL:

Identity still unknown. Security guards didn't see anyone escaping, but maybe somebody in Puddleford town center did? A shop owner or passerby?

MANESHA CHAUHAN, SUSPICIOUS SISTA:

Is winning the first challenge the perfect cover story? Maybe she stole it to use as a matching fashion accessory for the Sistas' glittery hoodies?

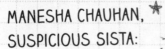

DARLENE DANGERFIELD:

Did she tell Give Us a Clue to get a grip when the Mustache disappeared because their getting upset made her feel really guilty about stealing it?

JESS DAVIES, GIVE US A CLUE: I'm not sure she is big enough to smash the display cabinet, or strong enough to carry away the heavy trophy, but appearances can be deceiving.

VERDICT: We can't accuse anyone of this terrible crime without more evidence. Our inquiry will continue to target two types of suspects:

belly button

tea

taffy

COMPETITOR TURNED BAD: We need to verify each contestant's bathroom break alibi,* ask about tea-drinking/ taffy-eating habits, and belly button hygiene.

OTHER CRIMINALS: Eyewitnesses must be sought who may be able to provide a description of any suspicious characters seen in Puddleford.

eyewitnesses sought

*ALIBI: A suspect can't be in two places at the same time. If it can be confirmed that he or she went to the bathroom and came right back, he or she can be removed from our suspect list.

Tuesday
August 7th

Who took the Mystic Mustache?

Breakfast

milk

coco Puffos

8:00 AM
BREAKFAST TABLE, MY HOUSE, 22 SYCAMORE AVENUE

Dad has just passed me this morning's *Puddleford Gazette* and the Young Super Sleuth's Society has issued a statement.

MISSING MUSTACHE OF MYSTERY!

Yesterday, the Young Super Sleuther Convention and Competition, being held in Puddleford Park, became a real-life crime scene, after the world-famous Mystic Mustache trophy was, we can now confirm, stolen.

Visitors were evacuated from the convention amid scenes of chaos.

Many were stuck in the parking lot for over two hours while security guards struggled to move a mobility scooter that had been stuck in a patch of mud.

Elle Lusive, top investigator and competition judge, has issued this statement on behalf of the Young Super Sleuth's Society:

"I'm pleased to say the convention site will open again today. However, to ensure that myself and Tartania are able to investigate, a number of changes will be introduced:

1. The Expect the Unexpected Challenge is canceled.

2. The Meet the Judges stand will be closed. (Signed photos of Elle and Tartania still available in the convention shop.)

3. Expensive detective gadgets on display have been removed for safe-keeping.

In the unlikely event the Mystic Mustache is not found, we would like to offer reassurance that the replica rubber trophies to be taken home by winners remain safely in the possession of the Young Super Sleuth's Society."

Should the so-called "best young detective agency in the world" have been able to stop a theft from right under their noses? Call our news desk with your opinions!

This is so frustrating! I don't think that Elle and Tartania should have canceled the Expect the Unexpected Challenge. What if people say that winning the competition was bogus because there  was no Mystic Mustache and that it was easier this year, so winners aren't really amazing detectives?

Even more frustrating, everything that happened yesterday makes it seem like the Young Super Sleuth's Society totally don't know what they are doing—which we know isn't true. That traffic jam wasn't their fault—it was whoever stupidly left that mobility scooter in a patch of mud!

FRUSTRATed

Without the Young Super Sleuth's Society
and advice from their informative Handbook, the
Mystery Girls would still be trying to solve the
Case of the Fuzzy Fish Finger.*

***THE CASE OF THE FUZZY FISH
FINGER:** One of our first,
very simple, mysteries. An
unexplained moldy fish
finger was found on the
floor of Mystery HQ.
We suspected Arthur
had put it there as a
joke, but after following
Young Super Sleuth advice
we uncovered evidence that
Watson (pet cat and trusty sidekick)
had been pulling things out of the Kitchen
garbage and hiding them for later in HQ.

moldy
fish
fingers

It's more important than ever that the Mystery
Girls help to restore the good name of the Young
Super Sleuth's Society.

9:30 AM
YOUNG SUPER SLEUTHER BACKSTAGE AREA

I should probably be worrying about the second
challenge, but we've been too busy.

When we arrived on-site, we kept our Mystery
Senses tuned in for further clues. The crowds are
smaller today and people look nervous, not excited
like yesterday. The balloon sellers aren't selling
golden mustache balloons anymore—they've been
replaced with black question mark-shaped balloons.
Quite fitting, since everybody is asking questions
about where the Mystic Mustache is and who
took it.

Backstage, we waited for the right moment to check bathroom alibis.

The Suspicious Sistas were practicing their Mystery Victory Dance for when they become Young Super Sleuther Champions. (Yeah, right.) I asked Manesha whether anything weird happened when she went to the bathroom during break yesterday. I watched carefully for signs that she felt guilty, but she just folded her arms and flashed Darlene an evil look.

"Weird? Only if you count spending the whole time arguing with Darlene Dangerfield," she said. "Darlene said her secret room was much better than our beach relaxation area. As if! Jess from Give Us a Clue kept telling us to stop fighting and be friends. Grow up!"

EVIL look

If Manesha was with Darlene and Jess in the bathroom for the whole break, none of them had a window of opportunity to steal the Mustache.

I have also observed that Darlene, Jess, and Manesha prefer fizzy jelly candies to taffies and none of them seem to drink tea, therefore we don't need to ask about belly button hygiene. We are crossing them off our suspect list.

jelly candies

That leaves the Bafflement Boys. They aren't eating taffies or drinking tea, but they are acting strangely. Even for them. They seem really jittery and they keep looking at their notepad and whispering.

"They are probably just preparing for the challenge, like they were yesterday," Violet said.

I don't know—maybe. HANG ON! NO WAY! CLUE ALERT!!

POPPY! VIOLET!

THIS IS NOT A DIARY ENTRY.
THIS IS A WARNING. DO NOT
LOOK AT THE BAFFLEMENT BOYS OR
YOU WILL GIVE AWAY THAT
I HAVE JUST LOCATED
INCRIMINATING EVIDENCE!!!

Bafflement mystery kit ↓

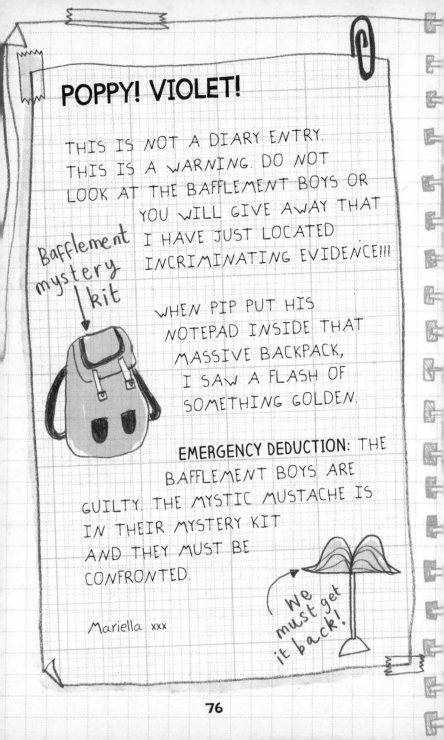

WHEN PIP PUT HIS
NOTEPAD INSIDE THAT
MASSIVE BACKPACK,
I SAW A FLASH OF
SOMETHING GOLDEN.

EMERGENCY DEDUCTION: THE
BAFFLEMENT BOYS ARE
GUILTY. THE MYSTIC MUSTACHE IS
IN THEIR MYSTERY KIT
AND THEY MUST BE
CONFRONTED.

We must get it back!

Mariella xxx

WHAT? Are you absolutely certain?! Let's tell an adult.

Violet x

adults

VIOLET! What are you talking about? I'll grab Linus. Violet—you grab Pip. Mariella—you grab their Mystery Kit!

Good luck, girls.

Poppy x

CRINGE ALERT! We might not be the brilliant detectives I thought we were.

"Why are you staring at us?" Linus said, as we waited to make our move. Pip folded his arms and glared at us too.

I gave Poppy and Violet a look that said, "Let's do this" and we raced toward them.

guilty?

Violet tripped over Give Us A Clue's Mystery Kit, but still managed to grab Pip's ankles as she fell. Linus tried to push Poppy away so she sat on his knee.

"You can drop the act, Bafflement Boys! We know you stole the Mystic Mustache and we know it's hidden in your Mystery Kit!" I said in my best I'm-a-serious-detective-who-has-lots-of-experience-in-this-type-of-crime voice.

Kiki shrieked in a really over-the-top way and hid behind Manesha and Dot. Elle Lusive and Tartania darted into the room. (Their mystery reactions are so quick.) Everyone else stared at us.

I grabbed the Bafflement Boys' Mystery Kit and almost toppled over. It weighed so much I could barely lift it. My heart raced. The Mystic Mustache was the only thing that could be making it so heavy.

Linus's arms waved uselessly from underneath Poppy. Pip tried to wrestle the bag from my grip, so Violet did the only thing she could from her position on the floor—yanked off his shoe and tickled his foot. Pip yelped, released his grip and the top of the backpack jerked open. There was the glint of gold and then . . .

THUD.

I stared at the object lying at my feet. It wasn't the Mystic Mustache. It was a set of golden false teeth.

false teeth

"Step away, Mystery Girl!"
Linus snapped at me as
he pushed a shocked
Poppy off his knee. "Just
because you didn't think
to search the crime scene
immediately after the theft
of the Mustache does not
mean you can attempt to
ruin our reputation or damage
important evidence!"

no mystic mustache!

WHAT?

Pip smirked and dropped the gold teeth back
into their Mystery Kit.

"Yeah, while you were sitting around having your little meeting, we were hot on the trail of the thief. We've already informed the judges who our suspect is," he said, raising his already perfectly positioned Mystery Eyebrow even higher.

"You may as well close your investigation, because it won't take us much longer to find the thief and return the Mystic Mustache, so WE can win it!" Linus said.

I realized then that they weren't racing off stage after the first challenge to see their moms—but because they were heading to search the crime scene. NO!

I wanted to say something clever, but all I could think of was, "*Little meeting?! We were following Young Super Sleuth procedure! Logical explanations always come before a search!*"

Pip rolled his eyes, as if to say that we were such amateurs.

"The Bafflement Boys have learned all there is to know about being a detective, so we make up our own rules," Linus said. "Now, if you could leave us in peace—we were in the middle of a top-secret mystery meeting."

He and Pip folded their arms and flared their nostrils smugly. They were totally enjoying how stupid the Mystery Girls looked in front of the other contestants—and, worst of all, in front of superstar detectives, Elle and Tartania.

massive nostrils

Right now, I'd like to disappear into the shadows, like Elle Lusive can—but I'm not a good enough detective to be able to do that. Just like I'm not a good enough detective to solve this case or to win this competition.

GIRLS

bathroom

3:00 PM
GIRLS' BATHROOMS, YOUNG SUPER
SLEUTHER BACKSTAGE AREA

I'm not a bad detective. The Clue Detection
Challenge we've just completed has proved that.

For the second challenge, each agency had to
search a cool, old-fashioned railroad car crime
scene. It was the sort of setting I've read about in
detective stories and it sent my Mystery Senses
into overdrive! I could tell Poppy and Violet were
just as excited as me by the
way they put aside feeling
embarrassed and
threw themselves into
searching for clues.

amazing

We totally would have won if the Bafflement
Boys hadn't found their stolen necklace
only seconds before we did. If we can
almost beat them in this challenge,
we can beat them in the next one.
And I've decided, they aren't
solving this mystery before we
do.

While the rest of the contestants are
having photos taken for a feature in the
Puddleford Gazette, Poppy, Violet, and I have
to go to the bathroom to discuss our next move.

"It's actually a good thing that we confronted the
Bafflement Boys—we can eliminate them from
our suspect list and we know about the false
teeth. That means we can try to figure out who
left them there and why," Poppy said.

"Yeah, at least my Mystery Senses were tuned
enough to spot that they had something golden
in their Mystery Kit," I said.

"You're right. The Young Super Sleuth's Handbook says that detectives who think they know everything always mess up, so we can't leave it to those Bafflement Boys to get the Mustache back," Violet said. "I can't believe they are making up their own detective rules!"

Totally. If we are going to do this, we must carry on the Young Super Sleuth's Handbook way—that's what has helped us solve all our other mysteries. In situations like this, the Young Super Sleuth's Handbook suggests looking again at the evidence. Then you have to decide your next step.

WHAT WE KNOW:

SUSPECTS: After ruling out the other contestants, we now know the thief must be a criminal who wants the Mustache because it's valuable, or because he or she wants to damage the Young Super Sleuth's Society's reputation, or both. But who?

NEW EVIDENCE:

A set of golden false teeth.

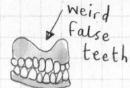

Weird
false
teeth

EXPLANATIONS FOR TEETH AT CRIME SCENE:

1. Could have been used to smash Mystic Mustache's display case— but why would the thief carry something as strange as golden false teeth?

2. Maybe the thief has stolen other golden objects and accidentally dropped the false teeth as he or she fled the scene, or couldn't carry it and the heavy Mustache at the same time?

3. Perhaps the thief wears false teeth? It's usually old people who have false teeth, but we've never seen a granny or grandad wearing a heavy set of solid gold teeth before. And would an elderly person be able to lift the trophy and escape?

CRAZY

OTHER USEFUL INFORMATION: The Bafflement Boys said they think that the thief is close by, which means they must have found

For Bafflement Boys' eyes only

some evidence to suggest this. What, though?

EXISTING EVIDENCE THAT MIGHT NOT MEAN ANYTHING: Belly button fluff, taffy wrappers, and tea used to disable alarm.

VERDICT: The golden false teeth have given us even more questions—and we need answers! Following up on our plan to seek out witnesses who saw anybody unusual struggling to carry a heavy object yesterday afternoon may help us to reveal the criminal's identity. We are also going to look at some of Poppy's books on famous criminals and crimes to see if any of their descriptions fit our suspect profile.

Missing Mystery Girl alert!

Violet just said something and it made Poppy go crazy.

"I know you'll think I'm nuts," Violet said. "Somebody like my granny would struggle to lift the Mustache—but the other evidence sort of fits with the idea that the thief is elderly, doesn't it? My granny wears false teeth and they fall out sometimes if she eats chewy taffies, and she has fluff at the bottom of her handbag, like the fluff we found. And she drinks lots of tea . . ."

"IT CAN'T BE!" Poppy shouted suddenly. Then she ran away!

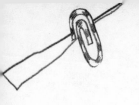

4:30 PM
YOUNG SUPER SLEUTH EXPERIENCE. HALL OF FAMOUSLY INFAMOUS CRIMINALS

We have just made a TOTALLY AMAZING BREAKTHROUGH!

Violet and I finally found Poppy in the Famously Infamous Hall of the Young Super Sleuth Experience Tent.

"Where have you been?" she said. Like we were the ones who ran away with no explanation.

"Um, looking for you!" Violet replied. "You ran away and didn't say where you were going."

"Didn't I?" Poppy said. "Never mind that. When Violet said how all the clues we'd found so far

pointed to an elderly suspect, I remembered
something I knew could be important, so I came
here to check it out."

Poppy pulled us past the life-size cut-outs of the
Diamond Diva and the Postal Pincher, toward
one of an old lady sitting on a sleek, black
mobility scooter printed with a swoosh of golden
stars. Her face was framed with shimmering
golden hair. She was wearing a fluffy
I'm-a-nice-old-lady cardigan, but
her piercing eyes gave me the
creeps.

"Meet the Golden
Granny," said
Poppy.

NAME: THE GOLDEN GRANNY (AKA ETHEL BOYSENBERRY)

AGE: 92

GOLDEN GRANNY FACTS:

Has been on the Young Super Sleuth's Society's Most Wanted list for over twenty years, since she retired from

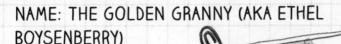

the golden granny

her job working in a jewelry shop and turned her love of golden trinkets into a life of crime.

*Has stolen valuables including a solid gold telephone, dog food bowl, and even a bathtub.

woof

*The Granny has outsmarted many detectives featured in the Young Super Sleuth Experience, including Elle Lusive and Tartania McSnuff, who joined forces to locate her after she stole a set of golden bagpipes.

GOLDEN GRIN: Wears a pair of solid gold false teeth, a treasured possession stolen from a dentist to Royalty. Uses her shocking smile to startle victims, before making off with their valuables. (She has strengthened her jaw muscles to be able to hold the teeth in place by chewing taffies.)

argh!

A GOLDEN GETAWAY: Old age and the weight of her jewelry means that the Granny is not able to make speedy getaways. She uses a high-speed mobility scooter to make her escape. Witnesses have reported her recklessly drinking a cup of tea while driving it. She has been known to drive her mobility scooter at full speed toward anyone who attempts to apprehend her.

VERDICT: All the evidence suggests that it was the Golden Granny who stole the Mystic Mustache! She is now on the Mystery Girls Most Wanted List!

No wonder Tartania and Elle looked so worried when the Mystic Mustache went missing—they probably realized right away that this was the work of the Granny and they should have been far more careful with the trophy. It won't be easy, but perhaps help from some fresh new detectives, like us (not the Bafflement Boys), will mean she is finally caught.

(That mobility scooter we saw yesterday was her getaway vehicle! I missed the golden stars because it was splattered with mud!)

She must be stopped

7:00 PM
MYSTERY HQ, MY HOUSE, 22 SYCAMORE AVENUE

We needed to make up for lost time, so it was tempting to start the hunt for the Granny immediately, but I knew that wandering around Puddleford hoping to bump into her wasn't going to work. The only way to track the Granny down was to have a plan more cunning than she'd proved herself to be.

"Now we know what the Bafflement Boys meant when they said they knew the thief was still in Puddleford," Poppy said. "The Granny can only walk slowly without her scooter and is carrying the Mustache, so she couldn't have gone far at all."

struggling

"Don't forget, though, she is a master criminal. She could easily have stolen another getaway vehicle by now," Violet said. "We need to check that Elle and Tartania have secured her scooter—if she's still in Puddleford, it might only be because she's waiting for an opportunity to get it back."

Violet was right. The Golden Granny might have already made her escape, before we even realized it was her we should be looking for.

"We don't know for sure she's still here. But we still need to think—where would a Golden Granny choose to lie low?" I said, hoping we weren't too late to keep her from getting away with the Mystic Mustache.

This is where we will target our search tomorrow. (While remaining vigilant for reports or signs of a Granny escape attempt):

POSSIBLE GOLDEN GRANNY HIDEOUTS:

TOWN HALL: They have a breakfast for seniors, so there would be a supply of tea and cookies in the kitchens for the Granny to survive on.

BAA-RMY YARN SHOP: Grannies like to knit, so the Golden Granny might be hiding in the stockroom and sleeping on piles of yarn?

BUS STOPS: Maybe the Granny won't risk trying to get her mobility scooter back and will instead attempt to leave Puddleford by bus? (If she hasn't already.)

All I can think about is how the Granny could be on a bus out of Puddleford right now, laughing her head off that she's outsmarted Elle and Tartania again. I bet she is thinking the Mystic Mustache will look really nice in her bathroom, right next to that golden bathtub she stole.

We can't let that happen. That's why, as well as our search, we'll put up these posters tomorrow morning.

HAVE YOU SEEN THIS GRANNY?

Known as the Golden Granny, she is suspected of stealing the Mystic Mustache and may be hiding in Puddleford.

Please report sightings to the Mystery Girls. (not any other detective agencies—they don't know what they are doing.)

DANGER!

Wednesday August 8th

NOTE: As we arrived at the convention I asked the security guards what happened to the mobility scooter abandoned yesterday. Puddleford police confiscated it—good! That's one less escape method for the Granny, but being a criminal genius, I'm sure she'll figure out another way. I just hope we aren't too late.

Bafflement Breakthrough Alert! (Argh! And yay!)

Even though we still hadn't sighted the Granny,
or found anyone who had (bus stops were clear
and there weren't any obvious signs that
BAA-rmy or Puddleford Town Hall had been
used as a hideout), we'd managed to get a lot
done. We put up all our posters around Puddleford
and I was feeling positive we'd hear from an
eyewitness soon.

eyewitness

Then, as we walked into the backstage area, I saw Pip elbow Linus, who rushed to fold away the big piece of paper he was inspecting. I read the words "GOLDEN GRANNY SIGHTINGS," so it must have been a map of Puddleford.

There were gold stars clustered around the center. One of them had THIS MORNING scrawled in big letters next to it!

GOLDEN GRANNY SIGHTINGS

THIS MORNING!

THE MAP

"Did you see that? The Granny is still in Puddleford! I can't believe we haven't had any reports yet and they must have ten sightings!" Poppy said.

I wished we had a map full of gold stars too, but at least if the Granny was still here we had a chance of catching her before the Bafflement Boys.

-gold stars

The Bafflement map also revealed some other very important information.

"We thought the Granny would be hard to spot, but she's popping up all over the place," I said. "I think this shows how desperate she is to find another getaway vehicle, something to replace her scooter!"

Poppy and Violet agree that this makes sense. Now that I think about it, catching the bus just isn't the Granny's style. It's far too slow, and if anyone saw she was traveling with the Mustache she'd be cornered.

cornered

BUS →

But what if she finds a new getaway vehicle in the next three hours? We can't stop her while we are busy competing in the third challenge! (Neither can the Bafflement Boys, which is good. But the Granny can't be allowed to leave Puddleford!)

10:15 AM
YOUNG SUPER SLEUTHER BACKSTAGE AREA, YOUNG SUPER SLEUTHER COMPETITION

Good news—the next challenge is going to be totally useful for tracking the Granny's movements!

"Two challenges down, two to go!" Elle announced, when all contestants were gathered on stage. "Now, Tartania, I've heard there have been reports of some very strange activity happening at Puddleford Library."

The Golden Granny, I thought. It's got to be! But Elle didn't mean that.

THE
GRANNY

"Aye, Elle, I think some Young Super Sleuther Surveillance might be required!" Tartania said. "For the next challenge, you'll be keeping Puddleford Library under close observation —spot the most incidents of suspicious activity and figure out what's really happening and you'll be the winner."

"Tartania and I will be in surveillance positions ourselves, filming your every move and reporting back to the audience," Elle said. "Good luck, competitors, you're going to need it!"

Excellent! I thought. If the challenge was going to be outside, we could watch for signs of the Granny at the same time. The Bafflement Boys raised their eyebrows at one another, clearly thinking the same thing. Poppy shot me a look that said, we'll show them.

1:15 PM
OUTSIDE PUDDLEFORD LIBRARY

I want to block the details of what just happened
during the Surveillance Challenge from my mind,
but the Young Super Sleuth's Handbook says a good
detective keeps a record of everything. I'm not sure
I'm a good detective anymore, but I'll write it down
anyway.

YOUNG SUPER SLEUTHER CHALLENGE AND
GOLDEN GRANNY SURVEILLANCE

10:20 AM: We find a hiding place in a large
hedge outside the surveillance target—Puddleford
Library. It also provides a good view of
other key areas of central
Puddleford, so it's excellent
for Granny-spotting.

10:45 AM: There is no unusual Super Sleuther or Granny-related activity, but we can totally see the other detective agencies' hiding places! Violet is sure that easy-to-detect surveillance positions are an instant point deduction. Darlene Dangerfield is sitting on a bench pretending to read a book; the Suspicious Sistas' bright-pink hoodies are visible in the upstairs window of Roll it Up carpet shop; Give Us a Clue thinks nobody can see them huddled behind a street sign; and the Bafflement Boys are crouching next to a tiny garbage can.

PUDDLEFORD TOWN CENTER

10:55 AM: Mrs. Finn from Fluff 'n' Feathers pet shop has just walked into the library. She is groaning and limping. Is that meant to be a clue or has she tripped over her pet poodle, Spangle, again?

Limping

11:00 AM: Violet starts searching the hedge we are in to check that the Golden Granny isn't hiding with us. It causes us to miss part of a distress signal being sent in flashlight beam flashes from the window of the children's library. All we manage to decode is, "INVASION, HELP!" What?

11:45 AM: Two more people limp into the library. Poppy thinks it might have been set up as an emergency hospital for people involved in a mystery incident. Hmmm. We need more clues.

11:57 AM: ARGH! High-pitched screams fill the air. My Mystery Senses leap into action. Give Us a Clue sprints from their hiding place.

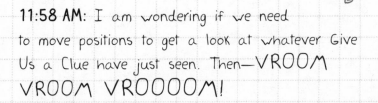

11:58 AM: I am wondering if we need to move positions to get a look at whatever Give Us a Clue have just seen. Then—VROOM VROOM VROOOOM!

11:59 AM: A huge sit-on lawn mower, with "Property of Puddleford Cricket Club" painted on the side, skids around the corner of the library. I don't need my Young Super Sleuth Binoculars to know who is hunched in the driver's seat, her curly golden perm bouncing wildly. The Granny has her new getaway vehicle!

12:00 PM: Before Poppy, Violet, and I have a chance to move, Linus from the Bafflement Boys throws his notepad at the Granny as she passes their hiding place. It lands, pages fluttering, on her face.

12:01 PM: The lawn mower bounces off the curb, swerves past the bush we are in, and out of view, down Puddleford Main Street. The Mystery Girls go after her. I see Linus following behind, but we've got a huge head start.

12:04 PM: CRASH! Turning the corner, we see the lawn mower upturned on a pile of squashed vegetables outside the Cabbage and Co. farm stand. Then we catch a glimpse of the Granny disappearing down the side of Soapy Suds Laundromat.

ARTIST'S IMPRESSION:

Shimmering hair. Hobbling, as if weighed down by her tangle of golden beads. Sparkling fluffy cardigan. Dragging wheelie shopping cart—is the Mystic Mustache inside?

12:10 PM: Poppy, Violet, and I stand at the top of the alleyway. There is a high wall at the other end and no sign of the Granny. Where did she go?

12:20 PM: After three searches of the garbage cans we realize it's no use and that we have lost the Granny.

12:25 PM: Back on the street, Elle Lusive is talking to Linus. I attempt to inform her of our Golden Granny sighting and near-miss in catching her, but Linus cuts me off and says that he's already told Elle that after we ran down the alley, the Granny reappeared further up the street, before escaping. Linus saw the direction she was headed and after studying his extensive list of sightings so far, he expects to track her down in the next few hours. NO!

12:26 PM: Feeling silly, the Mystery Girls turn to head back to their surveillance position, but Elle informs us that she actually came to find us because the challenge ended ten minutes ago and we came in . . . last! DISASTER.

NOTE: All the other contestants correctly identified that Puddleford Library was being invaded by ZOMBIES! (Well, Puddleford residents who had volunteered to pretend to be zombies.) That was why people were limping and groaning! Darlene Dangerfield won, and even though Linus chased the Golden Granny, Pip remained in position to watch the library!

SUPER SLEUTHER CHALLENGE OUTCOME: TOTAL FAIL

GOLDEN GRANNY SURVEILLANCE OUTCOME: SIGHTING CONFIRMED, BUT THOSE BAFFLEMENT BOYS ARE TOTALLY GOING TO CATCH THE GRANNY BEFORE WE DO! (ARGH!)

HQ

4:00 PM
MYSTERY GIRLS HQ, MYSTERY GIRL CRISIS TALKS

The Young Super Sleuth's Handbook says that when mystery-solving is not going according to plan or (as in this case) is a total disaster, you should hold an emergency crisis talk to assess what has gone wrong. That's what we've just done.

"Something weird is going on," I said. "One minute the Granny was hobbling around the corner, the next, she'd vanished! How did she do that?"

"Mariella," Violet said, "the Golden Granny is a master criminal who has evaded the capture of talented detectives like Elle Lusive and Tartania McSnuff for years. I don't think we should beat ourselves up about not being able to catch her."

"I agree," Poppy said. "We should let the Bafflement Boys find the Granny. They probably have already anyway, and we can focus on winning at least one of the challenges. It's not as good as becoming Super Sleuther Champions, but it would be better than going home as total losers."

Argh! I hate to say it, but I think Poppy is right. We'll never be overall winners now. Winning one challenge would put us in a tie situation with the Suspicious Sistas, the Bafflement Boys, and Darlene Dangerfield.

Total loser

So, it's decided. We are officially giving up on the search for the Mystic Mustache. Instead, we are going to concentrate on proving we aren't totally useless detectives by winning a challenge.

Maybe that will be enough to stop the Bafflement Boys' eyebrows going into smarty-pants overdrive when they win, solve the case, and become world famous. Maybe, but I really doubt it.

smarty-pants overdrive

determined

8:45 PM
MY BEDROOM, 22 SYCAMORE AVENUE

What was I thinking? The Mystery Girls should
be the ones to return the Mystic Mustache to
its rightful place—and not just because I want
to prove something to the Bafflement Boys.
The Mystery Girls never give up on mysteries
because they are stubborn!

The Bafflement Boys keep saying they are about to
catch the Granny, but are they really? I can't believe
I'm writing this, but it's actually something Arthur
did that changed my mind.

I'd thrown my artist's impression of the Mystic Mustache in the garbage, so I no longer had to be reminded of how I'd never win it or return it safely from the clutches of an evil granny. I was in a state that the Young Super Sleuth's Handbook calls Mystery Meltdown.*

*MYSTERY MELTDOWN: Extreme confusion when all you can do is lie on your bed and think about the silly mistakes you have made and seriously consider giving up being a detective.

There was only one thing that could cheer me up a little bit, and that was a chocolate bar from the Mystery Girl secret snack supply in HQ. (Clearly marked "Mystery Girl Treats: HANDS OFF, ARTHUR!") But when I picked up the tin, it felt very light—too light.

I may have been a bad detective this week, but I was still able to quickly deduce who was responsible for eating the tin's contents—ARTHUR!

empty!

I ran inside and flung open the door to Arthur's bedroom. He wasn't there. Then I heard the squeaky singing he does when he's using the bathroom and I was about to confront him in the bathroom when I spotted something on his bed.

Neatly laid out were three T-shirts. Each one was covered with a jumble of wobbly multi-colored little hearts and question marks drawn around photos of me, Poppy, and Violet.

T-shirts

I looked closer and realized they were photos from previous Mystery Girl investigations that brought back memories of mystery and adventure—and of how amazing it is to solve mysteries with Violet and Poppy. And how good at it we are!

Arthur must have made them for himself, Mom, and Dad when they come to support us in the audience tomorrow.

The amazing mystery Girls

I had the weird sensation that I wanted to hug Arthur. (Luckily it passed.) I knew then that I couldn't let the photo we took after the competition ended tomorrow be one of us all looking totally miserable because we had given up on the investigation. What sort of detectives would that make us?

I will, on this occasion, forgive Arthur for entering Mystery HQ, even though there was no need to eat our snacks while he looked for photographs. (I won't be this sappy and forgiving again.)

Good Luck mystery girls

Hmmm. Poppy made me and Violet good luck cards last night. Now I'm not sure I want to annoy her by saying I haven't given up on finding the Mystic Mustache after all.

* I know *
you'll be
EXCELLENT
as long as
you stay calm
and focused
and
WIN!
love POPPY
XXX

Thursday August 9th

Have the Bafflement Boys already found the Granny?

11:00 AM
GIRLS' BATHROOM, YOUNG SUPER SLEUTHER
BACKSTAGE AREA

I am a terrible Mystery Girl and a terrible friend.
I've let Poppy down by getting distracted by the
Granny—again!

On stage, Elle announced that the final challenge
was a Detective Disguise Challenge. Poppy
let out a sigh of relief. She is the Mystery Girl
Costume Coordinator and always makes
amazing disguises. Well, usually.

Detective Disguise Challenge

I spotted Linus glance into the shadows at the side of the stage, before narrowing his eyes and whispering something to Pip. What were they looking at? Had they already found the Mustache?

"MARIELLA!" Poppy shouted.

I turned to see that the curtain had lifted to reveal five dressing rooms. Whizzing through the air, suspended from hooks, were costume-making resources—sparkling fabric, disco balls, cool old umbrellas, and giant chunks of foam. Darlene Dangerfield narrowly beat Poppy to grabbing a roll of white sparkly fabric. Oh no. If Poppy hadn't shouted at me she would have gotten it.

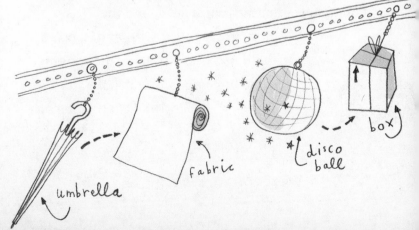

umbrella

fabric

disco
ball

box

The Bafflement Boys whisked
away cans of paint and some
giant fancy picture frames to their
dressing room. Kiki from
the Suspicious Sistas
skipped off carrying a
giant piece of cardboard.
(The sort of thing you could make cool
detective gadgets from.)

fancy frame

Paint

cool cardboard

One by one all the best disguise-making
equipment was claimed by the other competitors.
By the time I leaped into action, the most
interesting thing left was a big ball of purple
yarn. I thought it would be OK when I saw that
Violet had a mysterious-looking box. But it was
full of . . . twigs!

Poppy looked at the twigs, yarn, and the
boring brown fabric we'd ended up
with, shaking her head, though she
still managed to think of what
sounded like an ingenious
idea—tree costumes.

twigs

BORING fabric

yarn

She started wildly sticking and
cutting things, not in her usual genius
Costume Coordinator way, but in a panicking
under pressure type of way. The more Poppy
tried to fix things, the worse they got.

 Trees would normally be an excellent
undercover disguise, but there was no
way we were going to be able to sneak
up on suspects undetected in these.
Our trunks looked more like sausages
and our branches flopped around uselessly.

Things got really bad when the Suspicious Sistas
peeked out of their dressing room and giggled.
We saw that they were going to be three totally
cool, comfy, polka-dot armchairs. Darlene
Dangerfield (who was transforming herself into
a very convincing human statue) scoffed at us
and the Bafflement Boys, dressed as half-
finished masterpiece paintings—smirked.

Give Us a clue robots

Even though I was feeling really jealous of the other costumes, I was sure that we could fix ours.

Unfortunately, the pressure was too much for Poppy and she ran off of the stage. Poppy never gets upset, so we knew this was bad.

POPPY → upset

The Mystery Girls do not let members have Mystery Meltdowns alone. After I had one yesterday, I should have noticed she was close to the breaking point. If we can't do this together, we can't do it at all. That's why we went to help her.

Poppy is currently locked in a bathroom stall refusing to speak, but I'm not leaving until I know she is OK. (Or until she agrees to come back on stage because without Poppy's genius ideas, Violet and I aren't very good at making disguises.)

11:15 AM
OUTSIDE JUDGES' DRESSING ROOM, YOUNG
SUPER SLEUTHER BACKSTAGE AREA

WEIRD ALERT.

It took a while, but eventually, when I promised to focus, and Violet suggested that we should make simple bushes instead of trees, Poppy agreed to come out of the bathroom. That wasn't the weird part, though.

Leaving the bathroom, something I'd accidentally kicked bounced off the door of Elle and Tartania's dressing room. Looking down, I saw something catch the light.

A small golden bead.

golden bead

Then, when I looked up I
saw that the door handle of
Elle and Tartania's dressing
room was sparkling.

twinkle?

A closer inspection revealed that it was covered
with a thin layer of golden dust. I'd never seen Elle
or Tartania wear gold makeup before, so what
was this? Something else twinkled below—thin
strands of curled gold scattered on the floor. They
looked very much like strands of Golden Granny
hair.

Hair?

"Mariella, come on—these bushes aren't going to
make themselves!" Violet said from behind me.

I thought about ignoring the weird pieces of hair
and gold dust and following Poppy and Violet,
but a totally crazy thought entered my head.
Could the Golden Granny be hiding in Elle and
Tartania's dressing room?

I signaled to Poppy
and Violet for silence
and pointed to the
hair and the dust.

The idea that the Granny might be here reminded
me of something I'd read in the Young Super
Sleuth's Handbook.

"What if the Granny is using the oldest criminal
trick in the book?" I whispered. "What if she is
hiding right under the noses of those trying to
catch her because that's the last place she thinks
anyone will look? Or maybe she just came back
for her false teeth before she leaves?"

We are going in.

THE CUNNING CRIMINAL

Can't find your suspect? Think you've looked everywhere? Think again! Have you revisited the scene of the crime, the place you are sure your suspect must have fled from? If not, a suspect could be using one of the oldest criminal tricks in the book—hiding where you'd least expect them to!

Signs A Criminal May Be Closer Than You Think:

Depleted toilet paper supplies: Toilet paper may disappear much quicker than usual.

Giggling: Suspect may not be able to contain his or her excitement that he or she thinks he or she has fooled you.

Te he!

Creaky Floorboards: Could be a sign the suspect is wriggling to get comfy.

Crumbs: The criminal will need to eat.

Extra Squishy Sofa Cushions: Is the criminal concealed underneath?

Ways to Lure a Suspect Out of Hiding:

Sitting patiently

Sit quietly for a long time, thus fooling the suspect into showing himself or herself because he or she thinks you have left the crime scene.

Place a selection of pastries in an obvious place. Even a hardened criminal will struggle to find the willpower to resist the delicious smell.

YUM

Fling open closets and doors with no warning, leaving a suspect no opportunity to dart into his or her hiding place.

Evacuate!

Shout in a loud, clear voice:

"OH NO! The building demolition team is here."

WARNING

Do not suddenly throw open bathroom doors unless you are certain there isn't an innocent member of the public inside. This can lead to embarrassing situations and permanent damage to your mystery-solving reputation.

OPERATION GRAB THE GRANNY AND MISSING MUSTACHE

NOTE: Our mission took an unexpected turn at this point and I didn't get a chance to write everything down. This is an accurate account of events as they happened.

WARNING: Do not read if you are the sort of person that faints from shock.

Clothes rack

11:20 AM
DRESSING ROOM OF ELLE LUSIVE AND
TARTANIA MCSNUFF

Peeking into the room, I half-expected to see the
Golden Granny sitting with her feet up, applying
golden lipstick in Elle and Tartania's mirror. But
nobody was there.

"I don't like this!" Violet said from the doorway.
"We shouldn't be snooping! If we go back now
we can still make some half-decent ground."

Could the Granny be lurking behind the clothes rack
that was neatly hung with Elle's sparkling jumpsuits
and Tartania's plaid skirts? Behind
the chaise lounge in the corner?
Nothing stirred in the
shadows.

Chaise
lounge

"Maybe this is silly?" Poppy said.

I thought Poppy and Violet were right, but I decided to have one final check to make sure that the Granny wasn't under the table. Tartania and Elle's Mystery Kits were in the way. I tried to move Tartania's first and . . . ooomph!

It weighed a ton, just like the Bafflement Boys' Mystery Kit had when I found those false teeth.

Hmmm.

Opening the Mystery Kit of a world-famous professional detective without asking first would usually be a bad thing to do, but I just needed to know I wasn't going completely crazy.

"MARIELLA!" Violet shouted, "You can't do th—"

She didn't finish what she was saying because inside Tartania McSnuff's Mystery Kit was—the Mystic Mustache.

11:25 AM
DRESSING ROOM OF ELLE LUSIVE AND
TARTANIA MCSNUFF, STUNNED

We all stared. What was the Mystic Mustache
doing in the Mystery Kit of Tartania McSnuff?

"They got it back!" Violet said.
"Tartania must be saving it as a
surprise to give to whoever wins!"

"OH NO!" Poppy said, her eyes wide.
"We should have left the investigating up to
Elle and Tartania all along, then we could have
concentrated on winning it!"

Poppy and Violet must be right—and even though we wouldn't be the ones to win it, I thought at least the Young Super Sleuth's Society would be saved and, even better, Elle and Tartania had found the Granny and the Mustache without the help of the Bafflement Boys!

I leaned forward to zip the bag back up again, before something sticking out of Elle's Mystery Kit, on the floor next to Tartania's, caught the light.

It was a mass of tangled golden hair attached to some netting. A golden wig that looked exactly like Golden Granny hair. The Golden Granny didn't wear a wig, did she?

Wig →

The grins on Violet's and Poppy's faces turned to puzzled expressions as I pulled the zipper on Elle's bag fully open and saw that it was stuffed with the Golden Granny's fluffy cardigan, a shimmering skirt, and a pair of golden glasses!

"Professional detectives like Elle and Tartania would always put evidence like this into evidence bags," I said. "They wouldn't just shove it in their Mystery Kits."

"Maybe they haven't had a chance to sort it out yet?" Violet said. "Come on, we need to go!"

But how could we, when this was a totally unexpected and strange discovery? I pulled out a tangle of golden beads, like the ones we saw the Golden Granny wearing yesterday, except the beads weighed hardly anything. I realized that this wasn't just weird. It was suspicious.

"This stuff couldn't have belonged to the Golden Granny! The necklace is made of plastic!" I said.

"We were wrong about a few things with the Granny," Poppy said. "Maybe she doesn't always wear solid gold?"

Hmmm. The Granny has done a few surprising things so far—taking crazy risks popping up all over town, covering large distances without her mobility scooter—difficult when you are an old lady carrying a heavy golden trophy—so this could be true. I also thought that her being able to disappear from that alley when only moments before she was hobbling around was weird. But now she was wearing fake gold? It was almost as if she was a different Granny.

A different Granny.

A granny who could somersault over a wall.
A granny who could show herself, then blink-
and-you'll-miss-her-cartwheel disappear. A
granny who is not what she seems. Staring at the
contents of the two Mystery Kits on the floor, I
knew that we didn't just discover some nice
little surprise.

"We've been looking for the wrong suspect all this
time!" I said.

"Um, what?" Violet said.

I could hardly believe what I was about to say
myself, but that didn't make it any less true.

"What if the Granny has done some unusual
stuff because she isn't the Granny?" I
said. "What if the reason we saw Elle
Lusive, only moments after the
Granny disappeared yesterday,
was because the Granny *is*
master of disguise—Elle
Lusive?"

Elle
Lusive

Poppy clasped her hands to her mouth.

"Elle and Tartania stole the Mystic Mustache and made it look like it was the Golden Granny!" I said.

"Don't be silly!" Violet said. "Elle and Tartania are professional detectives. They wouldn't risk their careers, and the good name of the Young Super Sleuth's Society like this!"

Click, click. Click Click.

We heard the unmistakable sound of Tartania McSnuff's heeled boots in the hall outside.

"Hide!" I said.

There was just time to pull the zippers on the open Mystery Kits shut before Poppy, Violet, and I hid behind the chaise lounge.

WHEN GOOD DETECTIVES TURN BAD

Shocking as it seems, detectives can be driven by greed or revenge or arrogance and turn to a life of crime. Detectives have a detailed understanding of the criminal mind, making them some of the hardest criminals to catch. They know all the tricks to conceal their guilt.

Identifying the Rogue Detective:

Sneaks off to make "top secret" phone calls. Could be about an investigation or about a crime they are plotting.

A large backlog of unsolved crimes. Unsolved because he or she is the criminal behind them?

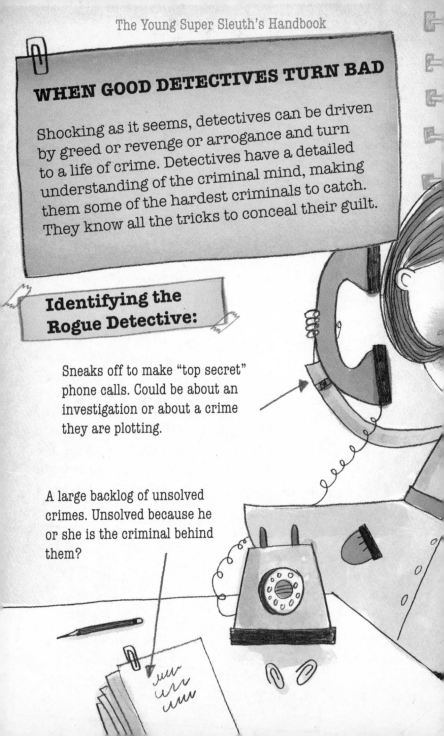

Squeezed between Poppy and Violet, I heard the swish of Tartania's heavy skirt and the door close behind her.

She flopped onto the chaise lounge like she didn't have a care in the world. I held my breath and willed Violet not to squeak and give away our position.

FUzzzzZZZ! Fuzzzzz!

There was a crackling sound—a walkie talkie—then Tartania spoke. "Are you in position, Lusive? I repeat, are you in position?"

FUzzzzZZZ! Fuzzzzz

"Affirmative. I'm ready," Elle's voice crackled. "My plan is working. Everyone believes that we've been called to investigate a suspicious incident on-site. Even better, the Bafflement Boys have taken the bait and are about to expose the truth!"

"Aye!" Tartania giggled. "Or what they think is the truth! If the Golden Granny could see us now!"

"Don't!" Elle snickered. "I might send a photo of myself in full Granny disguise to her in prison. I'm sure she'd love to see how she inspired us! It's perfect timing that the news we apprehended her hasn't been announced. Nobody suspects a thing."

GUILTY ALERT! I was right! Elle had just admitted to pretending to be a fake Granny and—unbelievable!—they didn't tell anyone they'd caught the real Granny so they could blame the whole thing on her!

Poppy was silently mouthing "No way" to me and Violet looked furious that we had been tricked by detectives we admired and had been trying to impress all week!

"Oh, stop!" Tartania said, laughing. "See you out there, Golden Granny! When I get back on stage I'll tell everyone we were called to a false alarm. The Mystic Mustache is on the move. Over and out."

Still chuckling to herself, Tartania heaved her plaid Mystery Kit off the floor, wobbled under its weight and shuffled out of the room.

We waited until her now unsteady footsteps had disappeared before we spoke.

"I . . . she . . . I . . . I can't believe she and Elle think this is funny!" Violet spluttered.

I knew how Violet felt. I'd been jealous that the Bafflement Boys seemed to know where the Golden Granny was. Now I felt sorry for them—by the sound of it, they were about to make a very public and very mistaken deduction.

"They've completely messed up our chances in the competition," Poppy exploded. "If they get away with this there will be no saving the Young Super Sleuth's Society. Not only did they allow the Mystic Mustache to be stolen, they didn't identify that their top detectives were to blame!"

"WE HAVE TO STOP THEM!" I said, racing from the dressing room. *run!*

We sprinted onto the stage, leaves flying from our half-finished tree costumes, just in time to see Linus grab the microphone from Tartania—his Mystery Eyebrow still clearly visible, even though his face had been painted to blend perfectly into the detective featured in his disguise.

"Please remain calm," Linus's voice boomed. "The Bafflement Boys have discovered . . . "

"STOP!" I yelled. They might be our arch-rivals but it was only fair to save Linus the embarrassment of getting things wrong.

The audience shifted their gaze from Linus to me, Poppy, and Violet. We looked as if we'd been dragged through a hedge, twigs sticking out of our hair and hanging uselessly from our shirts.

I could see Mom, Dad, and Arthur, all in their Mystery Girl support T-shirts, staring at me as if I'd totally lost it.

When I'd pictured what it would be like to be in the Super Sleuther final challenge, it wasn't anything like this.

The Suspicious Sistas, now three
sofas with only arms and legs
sticking out, put their hands on
their hips. Give Us a Clue turned
to stare (with great difficulty in
their stiff robot costumes). Darlene
Dangerfield rolled her eyes and
kept applying white makeup to
complete her frozen statue look.

Tartania stood, looking mildly surprised to see
us. She obviously thought she and Elle were
going to get away with the whole thing.

Poppy tilted her head slightly in the direction
of Tartania's Mystery Kit, letting me know it
was tucked at the side of the Suspicious Sistas'
dressing room. Good. Elle didn't make her
escape with the Mustache yet.

Even though this was
a tense situation, I had
the weird urge to laugh
when I saw that Pip was
dressed up to look
like an old-fashioned
lady detective. Pip did
not look as if he thought
this was funny; he looked
furious. Linus shot us a warning
glance that said, don't you dare
ruin my Big Reveal!

"As I was saying," he continued. "The Bafflement
Boys are pleased to announce that we have
tracked down the Mystic Mustache, which was
stolen by master criminal, the Golden Granny!"

There was a shocked gasp from the audience and
the other competitors.

"The Golden Granny is using the oldest trick in the book, hiding right under our noses, here on stage!" Linus said, looking smugger than ever, even though he had no idea what was really going on.

I didn't even feel the least bit smug that Linus was mostly wrong. I just wished the real Golden Granny had been behind this whole thing and that Elle Lusive and Tartania McSnuff could still be my heroes.

Pip pointed dramatically to a closed door in the wall at the side of the stage. We walked past that to get on stage and I assumed it must just contain props. I knew it definitely did not contain the Golden Granny.

mysterious door

GOLD
BEAD!

"Our attention
was drawn to this
concealed room
earlier, after a series
of golden beads
rolled from under the
door, like this," Linus said,
proudly pointing
to Pip, who was holding up one of the same
plastic gold beads we found earlier.

Tartania took a few exaggerated steps back from
the door. Now that I knew the truth, I could see
that she was faking it.

Poppy and Violet looked unsure what to do
next but I realized why beads had been rolling
out of that room. While Linus paused for
dramatic effect, I raced forward and grabbed the
microphone. (His detective reflexes were very
poor because it was easy.)

"The Bafflement Boys are wrong, but it's not their fault, they were tricked," I said in a rush. It wasn't really my best I-totally-know-what-I'm-talking-about voice, but I hoped everyone would believe me.

"Get lost, Mystery Girl!" Linus yelled. "You are just jealous because we found the Golden Granny first!"

Poppy and Violet tried their best to block his attempts to snatch the microphone back.

my best take me seriously face

"The Golden Granny is not in that room. Elle Lusive, disguised as the Golden Granny is," I continued. "Elle Lusive and Tartania McSnuff stole the Mystic Mustache and made it look like the Golden Granny took it!"

There was no gasp. Just a shocked, uncomfortable silence.

I glanced at Tartania McSnuff, who, weirdly, was now grinning at me. She clearly thought that by acting innocent, nobody would believe me. I waved at the plaid Mystery Kit by the side of the Suspicious Sistas' dressing room. Violet was there in seconds.

Grinning!

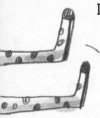

I pictured her lifting out the trophy and holding it up for everyone to see, but it was so heavy that all Violet managed to do was heave it out of the bag before she fell over backward.

The golden gleam of the Mystic Mustache was unmistakable, though! There was a sharp inhale from everyone in the audience.

"WHAT'S GOING ON?!" Darlene Dangerfield yelled.

"Unless I'm very much mistaken, Elle Lusive was about to run out of that room dressed as the Golden Granny before disappearing," I said. "That way you'd all believe that the Golden Granny had escaped with the Mystic Mustache and nobody would suspect Elle and Tartania are actually the thieves! When they were long gone you'd all find out that it couldn't have been the Golden Granny, because she is already in prison!"

I tried to fix my best don't-mess-with-me Mystery
Girl stare on Tartania, but it was hard to maintain
because she had started doing some sort of weird
Scottish dance.

"YIPPEEE!" she said, leaping from one foot to the
other.

What sort of deranged criminal were we dealing
with?

CRAZy

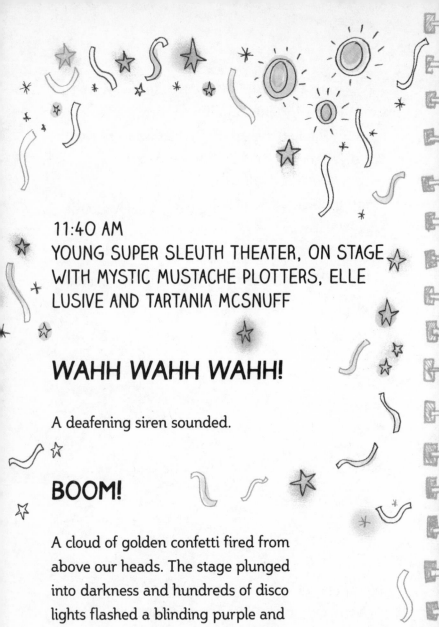

11:40 AM
YOUNG SUPER SLEUTH THEATER, ON STAGE
WITH MYSTIC MUSTACHE PLOTTERS, ELLE
LUSIVE AND TARTANIA MCSNUFF

WAHH WAHH WAHH!

A deafening siren sounded.

BOOM!

A cloud of golden confetti fired from
above our heads. The stage plunged
into darkness and hundreds of disco
lights flashed a blinding purple and
pink. Was this some sort of cunning cover
so that Lusive and McSnuff could escape?

The sirens fell
silent and the dancing
disco lights froze. I tried to get
my balance and, through the slowly
falling cascade of distracting confetti, I
saw the Golden Granny—or should I say,
Elle Lusive—in full golden costume,
cartwheeling toward Tartania from the
now-open door of the room at the
side of the stage.

Before I could attempt to chase her,
she flipped upright. She and Tartania
both looked totally excited, even though I'd
just destroyed their detective reputations.

My Mystery Senses told me something weird
was going on.

"Ah, Mystery Girls!" said Tartania, beaming. "We
can reveal that you have not been investigating a
real-life crime! You have actually been solving a
mystery set up by myself and Elle that was, in
fact . . ."

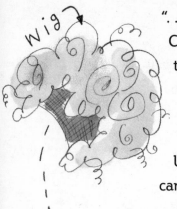

Wig

". . . The Expect the Unexpected Challenge!" Elle finished, throwing her golden wig in the air in celebration.

WHAT!? The Expect the Unexpected Challenge was canceled, wasn't it?

"This was our hardest Expect the Unexpected Challenge yet, because none of you knew it was happening," Tartania said. "We faked the theft of the Mystic Mustache and knew only the most daring detective agencies would attempt to open an investigation, taking their full concentration away from becoming Super Sleuther Champions."

Could Elle and Tartania be telling the truth?

"Well done, Bafflement Boys and Mystery Girls, for taking that risk. We set up a false trail leading, as you know, to the Golden Granny," Elle said.

"We expected some of you to guess that the Granny was the chief suspect, and maybe one or two of you to find where she was hidden," Tartania continued, beaming. "But even a fully qualified Super Sleuth would struggle to figure out that we were the ones behind the whole thing!"

"We would have told you the truth, of course, after the Bafflement Boys had exposed me," Elle said. "Congratulations to the Bafflement Boys for spotting those golden beads I was rolling under the door. And congratulations, Mystery Girls, for displaying some of the most advanced young detective work I have ever seen!"

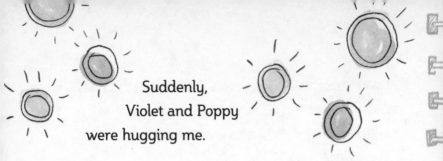

Suddenly,
Violet and Poppy
were hugging me.

"Did you hear what Elle said, Mariella?" Poppy
said. "Being a Young Super Sleuther is all about
thinking like a professional detective and that's
what we did!"

The audience had started clapping and cheering
now and I couldn't help smiling. This week had
been the most stressful ever, but I was relieved
that it was still OK to want to be just like Elle and
Tartania when I'm older. And actually, from what
Tartania said, we aren't that far off!

"So, hang on—there was never a Golden
Granny?" Linus said. For the first time, his
Mystery Eyebrow had fallen into the eyebrow
position of a normal person.

"Linus!" Pip shouted. He looked horrified and
was pointing madly at Linus's forehead.
Linus quickly repositioned something so his
eyebrow was back suspended near his hairline.

I could see now that all this time the perfect
Bafflement Boys' Eyebrows were just normal
eyebrows that had been stuck in place—with
sticky tape. Ha!

normal eyebrows

tape!

"Mystery Girls, you have been awarded
quadruple points for working out what Elle and
I were up to—and for having the courage to
confront us about it," Tartania said.

"And Bafflement Boys, you are the winners of the
Disguise Challenge!" Elle said. "Which means
that this year we have joint Young Super Sleuther
Champions!"

The audience clapped and cheered again and more golden confetti fell. Poppy and Violet jumped up and down. I could see Mom, Dad, and Arthur sitting in the front row, proudly showing off the T-shirts Arthur had made for people sitting nearby.

As I was still holding a microphone, this seemed like a good opportunity to give an excellent Young Super Sleuth Champion sort of closing speech.

But all that came out was, "ARRGGGHHHHEEEE! THE MYSTERY GIRLS ARE SUPER SLEUTH WINNERS! Oh, and so are the Bafflement Boys. YEAHHHHH!"

Oh well, I'd been working hard at being professional all week. Now it was time to PARTY!

chilling

3:00 PM
MYSTERY GIRL HQ, CHILLING ON A BEANBAG

When I woke up this morning I thought I must have dreamed all the amazing stuff that happened yesterday. Then I realized my pillow was covered in golden confetti that had been stuck in my hair and that my face felt numb because I'd rolled onto the rubber winner's Mystic Mustache trophy. (I'd fallen asleep holding it. Now that I've got it, I didn't want to let it go.) Conclusive proof that the best day of my detective career so far totally did happen!

Rubber replica!

After the cheering stopped, all
the contestants were whisked to
the Young Super Sleuth Experience
Famously Infamous Hall for a party. The exhibits
were pushed to the sides of the room, there was a
smoke machine set to maximum power
and a shimmering golden dance
floor. (Embarrassingly, Arthur
decided to start dancing
like a crazy person way
before anyone else did,
but I tried not to let that
distract me from the
amazingness of the
situation.)

embarrassing!

The Mystic Mustache glittered
as the disco lights reflected off it.
I couldn't believe the Mystery Girls were going
to have their names engraved on it—especially
since, just a few hours before, I'd been certain
we'd come last. It was such an unbelievable
feeling, I didn't even care that the Bafflement
Boys were joint winners.

The Suspicious Sistas came over and started high-fiving us, saying that if we wanted to we could definitely become Suspicious Sistas. I said thanks for the offer, but the Mystery Girls would be staying mysterious for now. (Forever, actually.)

Give Us a Clue didn't seem to care who'd won, not after they saw the massive buffet of mysterious golden food—golden mustache-shaped biscuits and egg salad sandwiches and sausage rolls!

golden biscuits

golden sandwiches

golden sausage rolls

You'd think the Bafflement Boys would have been more cheerful, but they just sat in the corner looking fed up.

Violet said that professional detectives (which we have proved we are) maintain good relationships with fellow mystery-solvers, even suspicious-smarty-pants annoying ones, and I knew she was right, so we went to speak to them.

Linus and Pip said congratulations and forced a smile. Then they said they'd been wrong to say the Mystery Girls would never be as good as the Bafflement Boys, because we officially were as good as them.

I really wanted to say that OF COURSE we are as good as them—actually, much better—but instead I said we'd let them know if there were any smaller cases we didn't have time to take on, because figuring out the whole Golden Granny mystery might make us world famous detectives in high demand. Ha!

World famous
mystery Girls

The best part of the whole party was when Elle and Tartania came over to congratulate us again.

Elle said the Mystery Girls had reminded her that a true Master of Disguise shouldn't cut any corners, and that she didn't know what she'd been thinking, wearing fake plastic golden beads and buying a cheap wig that shed hair. Then she winked and said that she knew who to call if she needed help with any investigations. WOW!

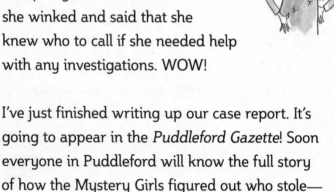

I've just finished writing up our case report. It's going to appear in the *Puddleford Gazette*! Soon everyone in Puddleford will know the full story of how the Mystery Girls figured out who stole— or didn't really steal—the Mystic Mustache.

CASE REPORT: THE MISSING MYSTIC MUSTACHE

The Mystic Mustache's theft was, in fact, staged by Young Super Sleuth's Society representatives, Elle Lusive and Tartania McSnuff, as part of a top-secret Expect the Unexpected Challenge, designed to test Young Super Sleuther competitors to the absolute limits of their mystery-solving abilities.

Elle and Tartania called a break after the first challenge, not so they could decide who had won, but so that they could stage the theft of the Mystic Mustache!

Unlike previous years, the Expect the Unexpected Challenge was far more difficult because everyone was led to believe that it had been canceled to allow Elle and Tartania to focus on finding out who took the Mustache.

Detective Sparks from Puddleford police is a huge
fan of Elle and Tartania's work, so he agreed
to go along with the investigation to make the
theft seem more convincing and to play a part
in training the next generation of detectives.

taffy

wrapper

The trail of strange golden clues we were
following—which we thought belonged
to the individual who'd stolen the
Mystic Mustache—were totally and
utterly fake. The trail pointed to the
Golden Granny—an infamous criminal
with an obsession for stealing all
things golden.

false teeth

tea

gold fluff

Elle Lusive disguised herself as the Golden
Granny, appearing in various places around
Puddleford. She lived up to her
reputation as a master of
disguise with a costume
and acting ability that
was almost flawless.
But "almost" isn't
good enough when the
Mystery Girls are around.

We were the only detective agency to notice that some of the Golden Granny's actions seemed odd, even for her, and we spotted clues Elle and Tartania never meant us to find. In her rush to get changed, golden beads, hair, and dust fell unnoticed from Elle's costume, just outside the judges' dressing room.

A search led to the discovery of the missing trophy and Elle's Golden Granny disguise. Closer examination revealed her golden jewelry was actually made from plastic. The Granny only wears real gold, so we knew it couldn't be hers.

Plastic

The only conclusion the Mystery Girls were able to draw was that Elle Lusive and Tartania McSnuff were mystery-solvers turned bad, and that it was them, not the Golden Granny, who had stolen the Mystic Mustache—and so we were faced with accusing our heroes of being criminals.

guilty

Even though our fellow young detectives (well, mostly the Bafflement Boys) thought we were totally crazy, we confronted Elle and Tartania and received quadruple points for not only following the false trail, but for being brave and professional enough to expose the truth—or what we thought was the truth.

innocent!
PHEW!

(It was an excellent way to practice our skills, revealing a dramatic scandal without actually having to see the reputations of our hero detectives ruined. YAY!)

CASE CLOSED.

NOTE: We've suggested to Elle and Tartania that they need to read contestant application forms more thoroughly in the future. They obviously didn't read the Mystery Girls' application form well enough—then they would have known that nothing gets past us! Plastic gold beads! What was Elle thinking?

This is the photo taken just after we won—it's our best Just Solved the Case photo yet! I might even get it printed on a T-shirt!

mystery Girl winners!

ACKNOWLEDGMENTS

I'd like to say a huge thank you to the people who have helped me live in a world of intrigue and fake mustaches while creating Mariella Mystery's world.

A massive Mystery Girl high five for my editor Jenny Glencross, who I have learned so much from and who always has a stunner of an idea in her Mystery Kit. I'm grateful for her time, patience, and commitment to Super Sleuthing.

A top-secret handshake for the team at Orion for their support, enthusiasm, and hard work in making Mariella an international mystery solver. Mystic Mustache awards also go to my agent, Mark, for starting me on this amazing journey and to my husband Simon, for helping to clear my brain of red herrings and being very understanding that a detective's work is never done.

This message will self-destruct in five . . . four . . . three . . . two . . .